Dear mouse friends,
Welcome to the world of

Geronimo Stilton

THE RODENT'S GAZETTE
EDITORIAL STAFF

Geronimo Stilton
A learned and brainy
mouse; editor of
The Rodent's Gazette

Thea Stilton
Geronimo's sister and
special correspondent at
The Rodent's Gazette

Trap Stilton
An awful joker;
Geronimo's cousin and
owner of the store
Cheap Junk for Less

Benjamin Stilton
A sweet and loving
nine-year-old mouse;
Geronimo's favorite
nephew

Geronimo Stilton

FIELD TRIP TO NIAGARA FALLS

Scholastic Inc.

Copyright © 2005 by Edizioni Piemme S.p.A., Palazzo Mondadori, Via Mondadori 1, 20090 Segrate, Italy. International Rights © Atlantyca S.p.A. English translation © 2006 by Atlantyca S.p.A.

The publisher does not have any control over and does not assume any responsibility for author or third-party websites or their content.

GERONIMO STILTON names, characters, and related indicia are copyright, trademark, and exclusive license of Atlantyca S.p.A. All rights reserved. The moral right of the author has been asserted. Based on an original idea by Elisabetta Dami.

geronimostilton.com

Published by Scholastic Inc., *Publishers since 1920*, 557 Broadway, New York, NY 10012. SCHOLASTIC and associated logos are trademarks and/or registered trademarks of Scholastic Inc.

Stilton is the name of a famous English cheese. It is a registered trademark of the Stilton Cheese Makers' Association. For more information, go to www.stiltoncheese.com.

ISBN 978-0-439-69146-8

Text by Geronimo Stilton
Original title *In campeggio alle cascate del Niagara*
Cover by Iacopo Bruno, Roberto Ronchi, Mirka Andolfo, and Laura Dal Maso
Illustrations by Larry Keys, Ratterto Rattonchi, and Chiara Sacchi
Graphics by Merenguita Gingermouse

Special thanks to Kathryn Cristaldi
Translated by Lidia Morson Tramontozzi
Interior design by Kay Petronio

OH, HOW I HATE BEING LATE!

"Rain, rain, go away." It was the middle of the night. I was in my comfy, cozy bed, trying to sleep. But the rain was beating on my window like a crazed woodpecker.

I fell asleep dreaming about birds and pounding ocean waves and huge crashing **waterfalls**.

It rained the whole night. The next morning, I woke up exhausted. I stared at

Rain, rain, go away!

the clock on my bedside table. Holey cheese! I was **late**! Oh, how I hate being **late**!

I hurled myself into the bathroom. I turned on the shower while brushing my teeth. I combed my whiskers while pulling on my pants. I chugged down my coffee while racing out the door. Rats!

I ran at *BREAKNECK SPEED* to my aunt Sweetfur's house. That is where my little nephew Benjamin lives. I had promised to take him to school today.

Benjamin giggled when he saw me. I had forgotten to button my pants. And my fur was sticking up all over the place.

On the way to school, we passed by my office. I run the most **FAMOUSE** daily newspaper on Mouse Island. It is called *The Rodent's Gazette.*

I turned on the shower while brushing my teeth!

I combed my whiskers while pulling on my pants!

I chugged down my coffee while racing out the door!

Benjamin tugged on my paw. "Uncle, may I take my friends to visit you at the *Gazette* sometime?" he asked.

I s**m**iled. My nephew was such a sweet and smart little mouse. Maybe someday he would follow in my pawsteps and run a newspaper, too.

"Of course, dear nephew," I said.

Finally, we arrived at Benjamin's school. **WHAT A ZOO!** Little rodents were running everywhere. Some held on to their parents' paws. Others tumbled off the school bus. Some zipped up on bicycles. It was so loud I could barely hear myself squeak.

Just then, the school bell rang. Rrrrrrrrrriiiiiiiinnnnnnnnnnnnnnnggg!

I nearly jumped out of my fur. And that was when I spotted a *blonde* rodent. No, she wasn't just any blonde rodent. She had **GORGEOUS** fur. She had a **SWEET** smile. And she had **blue** eyes the color of a clear summer sky.

"Good morning, I am **Miss Angel Paws**, Benjamin's teacher," she said.

I took a step toward her. But before I could shake her paw, I tripped over my tail. I landed snout first in the dirt.

BENJAMIN'S FRIENDS

Liza

Punk Rat

Kenny

Kay

Scampers

Mohamed

Sam

Carmen

Shannon

Malcolm

David

Esmeralda

Lucy

Beth

Laura

Susan

Steven

Antonia

Tim

Sakura

Benjamin

Oliver

DON'T WORRY ABOUT A THING!

I turned to run away with my tail between my legs. I was so embarrassed. Why did I have to make a fool of myself in front of such a PRETTY mouse?

"Today, we'll decide where to go on our field trip," I heard Miss Angel Paws announce.

Hmm. Field trip. Suddenly, I had an idea. Maybe the class could come visit me at *The Rodent's Gazette.* Then the teacher would see I wasn't just a clumsy, dim-witted mouse. I strode back into the classroom.

"Oh, good, Mr. Stilton, you haven't left. I wanted to ask for *your advice*," Miss Angel Paws squeaked. "Do you think this is a good place to go on a field trip?"

She began writing something on the blackboard. I would love to tell you what it said, but I couldn't read it. No, it wasn't written in ancient Squeakeeze. I just couldn't see a thing. That's because the class bully, Punk Rat, **had tripped me** on my way in. I had lost my eyeglasses.

The teacher **tapped** on the board. "What do you think, Mr. Stilton?" she repeated.

I squinted desperately at the board. I felt like one of the three blind mice.

Everything looked FOGGY. Then I **thought** of something. Maybe Miss Angel Paws wanted to visit *The Rodent's Gazette*. Maybe that's what she had written on the board. Yes, that had to be it, I decided. That's why she wanted my advice.

"I think that's a great idea!" I said to the teacher. "I would love to take you there!"

Miss Angel Paws was amazed. "Really, Mr. Stilton?" she squeaked.

"Of course," I said. "And don't call me Mr. Stilton.... Call me Geronimo!"

"But who will pay for it? When can we go? Don't you have to work?" asked the teacher.

"Don't worry about a thing," I told her. "I can take a little time off. You will all be my guests. We can go today *if you'd like.*"

The teacher squealed with delight. She clapped her paws together. "Guess what, class? Mr. Stilton—I mean Geronimo—has volunteered to take all of us to *Niagara Falls* for a whole week!" she announced. "We'll leave today!"

The class **CHEERED**.

"Hooray! We're going to Niagara Falls! Thank you, Mr. Stilton!" they cried.

I blinked.

"Niagara Falls?"

Punk Rat pulled at one of my whiskers.

"Of course. Can't you read? Look at the blackboard," he smirked, handing me my glasses. I put them on. I stared at the blackboard. It read **CLASS TRIP TO NIAGARA FALLS**.

I gulped. Oh, how did I get myself into **such a mess**?

The teacher was already calling the travel agency. "Yes, twenty-two students, a teacher, and Geronimo Stilton. We need **twenty-four** round-trip tickets to Niagara Falls," she squeaked into the phone.

What could I do? The class was so **excited** they could hardly sit still.

With a sigh, I took out my credit card. It's a TOP MOUSE Diamond-Plus-Super-Deluxe-Extra-Supreme-Gold Card. It was a good thing I had it. This trip was going to **cost** me more than my two-year subscription to the Cheese-of-the-Month Club!

After booking our trip, the teacher waved a yellow notebook in the air.

"Class, this notebook will be our TRAVEL JOURNAL," she announced. "We will write in it every day. That way, we will never forget this wonderful trip."

THIS IS HOW TO KEEP A TRAVEL JOURNAL.

TODAY IS: ....

WE PLAN TO VISIT: ....

THE WEATHER IS:

☐   ☐   ☐

WE SAW: ....

....

WE REALLY ENJOYED: ....

....

WE ATE: ....

....

WE LEARNED: ....

SURPRISES: ....

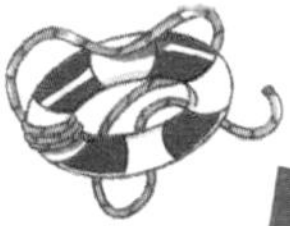

....

Paste a
photo of
this day
here!

THIS PHOTO WAS TAKEN AT:

....

ARE WE THERE YET?

Do you know how to get to Niagara Falls? Let me tell you. The falls are located at the border of the United States and Canada. They are very far from Mouse Island. The flight was the longest one of my life. Well, OK, maybe it wasn't the longest, but it was the **WORST**. That's because ...

Scampers spilled orange juice on my computer ...

Sakura smeared ice cream on my tie ...

David pulled out one of my whiskers ...

Scampers spilled **orange juice** on my computer.

Sakura smeared **ice cream** on my tie.

David pulled out one of my whiskers.

Carmen knocked down my suitcase.

Esmeralda *squeaked my ear off*.

Tim asked me **317** times, "Are we there yet?"

The whole time I tried desperately to read my book on Niagara Falls.

Tim asked me 317 times...

Carmen knocked down my suitcase...

Esmeralda squeaked and squeaked...

NIAGARA FALLS

Located at the border of the United States (on the east) and Canada (on the west), the falls are formed by the waters of the Niagara River. During the journey from Lake Erie to Lake Ontario, the river suddenly drops more than 180 feet to the level of the riverbed, forming falls unique in their power.

There are actually two different falls at Niagara. On the Canadian side there is Horseshoe Falls, approximately 2,200 feet wide, while American Falls, on the American side, is approximately 850 feet in width.

In the winter, the river freezes, but the falls do not because they are in continuous movement.

Every second, more than 760,000 gallons of water fall!

Niagara Falls is also a precious source of electrical energy. Approximately 50 percent of the water (at night and during the off season, 75 percent) is directed to the hydroelectric power plants that supply the United States and Canada with electricity.

But the power of the water is creating a problem for the future of the falls. In the past 12,000 years, the water running over the rocks has eroded them and shifted the falls by almost seven miles.

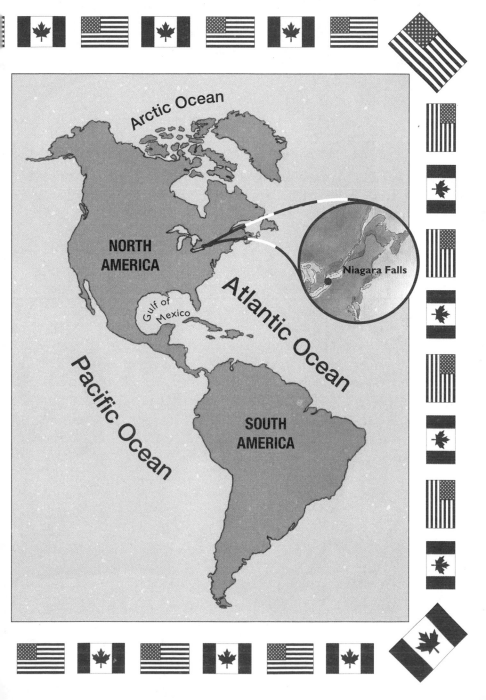

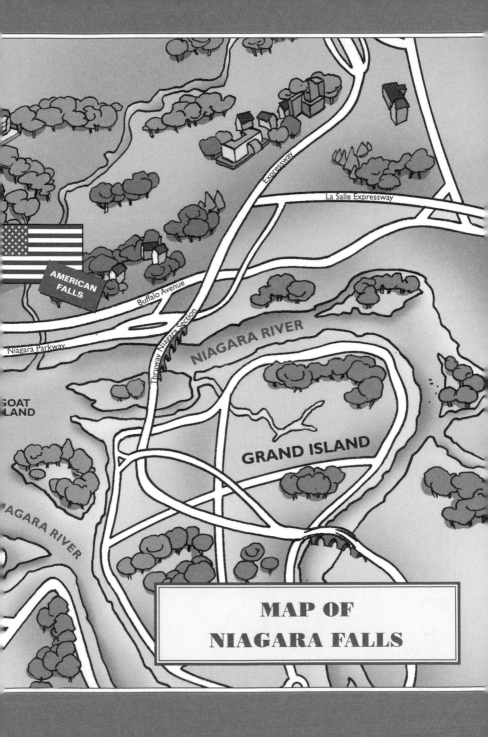

A BIT OF HISTORY . . .

THE ERA OF EXPLORATION

For thousands of years, only the Indigenous peoples who lived at what is now the border between the United States and Canada knew about the spectacular falls. The first written record of their existence dates back to the second half of the sixteenth century. The man who made them famous was Louis Hennepin, a Belgian monk who was part of an expedition organized by the French explorer René-Robert Cavelier, Sieur de La Salle. The expedition arrived at the falls in December 1678, and its members were mesmerized by their size and grandeur.

At that time, the falls had a drop in level of more than 590 feet and carried twice as much water as they do now.

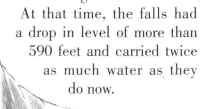

THE FIRST TOURISTS

Tourism was slow to arrive. One of the first important visits by Europeans occurred in 1791, when the duke of Kent (father of the future Queen Victoria of England) stayed at the only building in the area: a small wooden hut!

The first groups of European tourists began arriving during the mid-1800s. The falls continued to attract important guests, such as Jerome Bonaparte, brother of the famous Napoleon. He came from New Orleans on his honeymoon. From that moment on, Niagara Falls became a popular destination for couples on their honeymoon.

EVERYONE,
EXCEPT ME!

Just before our **plane** landed, the captain made an announcement.

"**Attention**, rodents: We are now passing over the famouse Niagara Falls. Take a look out your window if you would like to see a truly spectacular view of the falls," he advised.

Everyone wanted to see the falls.

Everyone leaped to the window.

Everyone saw the spectacular view.

EXCEPT ME! EXCEPT ME! EXCEPT ME! EXCEPT M

EXCEPT ME!

I was being suffocated by a throng of screaming, jumping mouselets. They had **PRESSED** themselves up against my window. I couldn't move. I couldn't breathe. I couldn't see a thing!

Finally, the plane landed. We were in Toronto, Canada. From there, we climbed on a **bus**. We rode on the bus for about **an hour and a half**. Then we arrived at the falls.

As we pulled up, the driver made an announcement: "**We have now reached the famous Niagara Falls. Look out your window if you would like to see a truly spectacular view of the falls,**" he said.

"Look at the falls!"

Everyone wanted to see the falls.
Everyone leaped to the window.
Everyone saw the spectacular view.

EXCEPT ME! EXCEPT ME! EXCEPT ME! EXCEPT ME! **EXCEPT ME!**

A throng of **screaming** mouselets was

crawling all over me. They plastered themselves up against my window. I couldn't move. I couldn't breathe. I couldn't see a thing!

The bus stopped. I got off. The ROARING SOUND of the falls was incredible.

I tried to take a picture.

Everyone wanted to take a picture of the falls.

Everyone got his or her camera ready.

Everyone snapped away at the falls.

EXCEPT ME!

Oh, if only I could get away from those screaming mouselets. They were all over me! I couldn't move. I couldn't breathe. I couldn't see a thing!

The bus took us to the city of Niagara Falls. It was already dark.

EXCEPT ME!

I Do Not Know How to Set Up a Tent!

What a day! I was tired. I was **hungry**.

I **STUMBLED** off the bus. I couldn't wait to sink into a nice **SOFT** bed. I couldn't wait to put on my fluffy cat-fur slippers. I couldn't wait to order from room service.

"Is the hotel nearby?" I yawned. "I'm pooped."

Miss Angel Paws looked shocked.

"Hotel? Why, Mr. Geronimo, we have come to enjoy the great outdoors. We're not going to a hotel. We're going to **CAMP OUT**," she squeaked.

My eyes opened wide. I looked around. Miss Angel Paws wasn't joking. We were standing in the middle of the wilderness!

Did I mention I'm not much of an outdoor mouse?

"Um, yes, well, who's going to set up the tents?" I stammered.

Miss Angel Paws rolled her eyes.

"You are, of course, Mr. Geronimo," she said.

I made a *quick* calculation: There were **twenty-four** of us. Each tent would hold **four** mice. That meant I had to set up **six** tents for the little mice. Then we would need **one** tent for me and **one** for **Miss Angel Paws**. Plus, we needed **one** big tent for all of us to eat breakfast in.

Holey cheese! I couldn't set up **nine tents**!

Just then, the little mice began whining. "Come on! We're tired!"

I couldn't make heads or tails of the tents.

I set up one tent inside out. I zipped myself up in another and couldn't get out. Then I whacked my paw with a hammer.

"I give up!" I **screeched**.

Did I mention I'm not much of an outdoor mouse? I sat down on a rock. I took off my glasses so I could SOB FREELY. **"Help! I can't do this!"**

Just then, my little nephew Benjamin whispered in my ear.

"Call Aunt Thea. She always knows what to do," he suggested.

I dried my tears. "Good idea," I agreed. I guess you could say my sister, Thea, is the opposite of me. She loves a challenge.

A half hour later, after I talked to Thea on the phone, all of the tents were ready.

"Hooray!" yelled the little mice.

"Isn't it great sleeping in a tent, Mr. Geronimo?" Miss Angel Paws said.

HOW TO SET UP A TENT

1

Lay the tent flat and stake the corners.

2

Assemble the frame by connecting the poles, and hook the tent to the frame.

3

Pull the lateral ropes and stabilize the tent by staking the ropes.

4

Mount the rain tarp and attach it well with the stakes.

5

Drainage ditch for water runoff

Dig a drainage ditch around the tent. You'll need it in case of rain.

Where to Set Up a Tent

NO

NO

NO

YES

Choose a flat area or one on a gentle slope that is well protected from the wind.

I Do Not Know How to Cook at a Campsite!

I was so tired I could only nod. Then I heard a low grumble. Was it a bear? Was it a fox? Was it a **RAVENOUS**, rodent-eating monster? No, it was just my tummy. I was starving!

"So, **who will do the cooking**?" I asked.

"Why, you will, of course, Mr. Geronimo," Miss Angel Paws **said**.

The little mice began screaming.

"come on! We're starving!" they whined.

I sighed. I trudged to the brook to get some w. a t e R. But on the way back, I tripped. The water flew out of the bucket.

I decided to get the FIRE started. But the wood was too damp. It would not light.

I went to get some more wood and accidentally stepped on the egg carton. CRUNCH!

Then I noticed an army of ants. They were devouring all of the bread.

"I give up!" I squeaked. Did I mention I'm not much of an outdoor mouse?

"Try calling Aunt Thea again," Benjamin whispered. "She'll know what to do."

A half hour later, the fire was ready.

Now if I could just get the ants off the bread. . . .

HOW TO COOK OUTDOORS

Before you light a fire, find out the wind's direction. Always be aware of the danger of fires! Keep a bucket of water nearby to put out the fire and always get help from an adult.

Tripod

Bind three wooden poles together. Then hang a pot on a chain that has been secured at the top of the poles.

Flat rocks

Arrange several clean, flat rocks so they are heated by a fire underneath. You can cook eggs, fish, or meat on top of them.

Forks

Arrange two forked sticks across from each other on either side of the fire. Hang the pots on a strong piece of wood, and then place each end of the wood in the forks.

Never Leave Fires Unattended!

COME ON!
WE HAVE TO GO!

After we ate, I fell asleep with my snout in my plate. I woke up with a start.

"Psst, psst, Mr. Geronimo!" a voice called.

It was **Miss Angel Paws**.

"Mr. Geronimo, you, um, forgot to set up a bathroom," she whispered.

I paled. A bathroom?

"Come on! We have to go!" the little mice squeaked.

This time, I knew exactly what to do. I called my sister. I wasn't proud. I was desperate. After all, who knew how to set up a bathroom outdoors?

Of course, my sister figured it out.

Half an hour later, the bathroom was finished. And so was I. I crawled into my sleeping bag and slept like a ten-ton brick of stale cheese. Even a starving mouse couldn't have moved me.

Ronfff...bzzz...ronfff...bzzz...ronff...

THE TOILET

HOW TO MAKE A BATHROOM

Toilet **1.**

1. Dig a hole. Leave a big pile of dirt next to the hole. After each use, throw some piled-up dirt into the hole.

2.

2. Use some wooden poles and a tarp to build a screen around the toilet.

3. Shower

3. Build a tripod. Hang a bucket with water to use as a makeshift shower.

Sink **4.**

4. Build another tripod. Place a bowl on top to wash your paws and snout.

WHAT A STINK!
WHAT A SMELL!
WHAT A STENCH!

I woke up in the middle of the night. An AWFUL stench surrounded me. It smelled worse than my cousin Trap's rancid fish soup. IT SMELLED WORSE THAN MY GRANDMOTHER ONEWHISKER'S DISGUSTING BRUSSELS SPROUT SOUFFLÉ.

I opened my eyes. A black-and-white furry creature with two beady little eyes stared back at me.

I jumped out of the sleeping bag, **squeaking** at the top of my lungs. FLASHLIGHTS snapped on all over the campsite.

"**What a stink**!"
"**What a smell**!"
"**What a stench**!" I heard the other campers CRY.

I couldn't have agreed more. I started to chime in when I heard some more voices.

"Where is it coming from?" one said.

"That tent there," another answered.

"That's the rodent from New Mouse City. The one named *Geronimo Stilton*," a third cried.

"He really needs to clean up his act," someone else piped up.

"Yeah, I wonder if he knows what the word 'bath' means," another muttered.

I turned beet red. How could they talk about me that way? I'm no **sewer** mouse. I love taking baths.

But there was no time to think about a bubble bath now. I had to defend myself. "I'm not the **stinky** one," I started to explain. "It was that creature. It had **BLACK** fur with a **WHITE** stripe..."

Punk Rat snickered. **"What creature? I don't see any creature,"** he smirked.

Punk Rat

Then he began to sing in a high-pitched voice: **"Geronimo sees things in the dark. A slug, a squirrel, a giant shark!"**

Benjamin grabbed my paw. "Uncle, did you really see a creature?" he whispered. When I nodded, he stuck his snout in the tourist guide. I guess he was pretending he didn't know me. I couldn't blame him. Everyone thought I was losing my whiskers.

At that moment, Benjamin began squeaking. He held up the book. It showed a picture of the creature.

"See, my uncle was right!" my nephew told Punk Rat. "The creature he saw is called a **SKUNK**!"

A skunk is a mammal in the weasel family. It has a thick black coat with white stripes. It lives in woody areas and feeds on insects, small mammals, and fruit. To protect itself from predators, it uses a unique system: It raises its tail, spreads its hind feet, and sprays a smelly liquid that it can send as far as twelve feet.

A Wall of Rushing Waters

The next morning, we woke up at dawn. After breakfast, we hiked along the river.

I was tired. You probably already know that I am not a morning mouse. **But I was also excited.**

Finally, I would be able to see Niagara Falls!

Our paws crunched through the thick autumn leaves of yellow, red, and **brown**. The air smelled crisp and fresh. Don't you just love autumn? I do. I love everything about it. Oh, except for Halloween. I'm not big on scary holidays.

I started thinking about the Halloween

...a magnificent

party my cousin Trap was throwing this year.
He said he was going to dig up a real skeleton
and serve frozen eyeballs for dessert!

Just then, I felt like my own eyeballs had
frozen. Well, my eyeballs and the rest of my
body, that is. I was staring at a tremendous
wall of rushing water. We had reached the
falls! The river rumbled like thunder.

rainbow...

A magnificent rainbow made a bridge over the falls.

Ah, what an unbelievable sight! I could have stood and admired the falls all day. I just had one little problem: The rushing water was getting to me. With a squeak, I took off in search of a bathroom.

ALL ABOARD!

A few minutes later, I was back at the falls. Miss Angel Paws was making an announcement.

"We will now board a boat called the *Maid of the Mist* that will take us to the falls," she told the class. "Please do not lean over the side."

We put on shiny raincoats. Then we climbed aboard the boat.

MAID OF THE MIST IV

It sailed straight up the Niagara River. Everything looked so different from BELOW.

A mist rose **UP** from the *spraying* water. We were SO close to the falls.

I dug my paws into the railing of the deck. The water **churned** below us. I was glad we were all safe on the boat.

The sprays of water soaked my fur. Oh, well. No one could say I was stinky now.

I looked around. We were surrounded by fog.

A VISIT TO THE FALLS

The experience on board the *Maid of the Mist* is a very damp one, since the ship, navigating through sprays, goes right to the base of the falls. It is a breathtaking trip, and one of the best ways to appreciate the strength of this enormous body of water.

I felt like I was in a dream.

Just then, I remembered a story that I had read about Niagara Falls. I told it to the class.

A long, long time ago . . .

THE LEGEND OF THE MAID OF THE MIST

There was once a beautiful maiden named Lelawala. Her father promised her hand in marriage to a king. But she did not love this king; her heart belonged to He-No. He-No was the god of thunder and he lived in a cave under Horseshoe Falls. One day, as Lelawala was paddling a canoe onto the Niagara River, she decided she could not marry the man her father had chosen for her. Soon she was swept over the falls. He-No, who had been watching his true love, saw this. He stretched out his arms and saved Lelawala just as she fell. It is said that their spirits still live in the cave beneath the falls.

DON'T MOVE, PUNK RAT!

When I finished telling the STORY, I looked up. The boat was returning to shore. Right then, I noticed something. It was quiet. Too quiet. I began to get the feeling that something — or someone — **was missing**.

I ran up and down the boat counting the little mice.

"One two three four five six seven eight..."

I was right. We were short one rodent. **Can you guess who was missing?** Here's a hint: He's the loudest mouse in the class and a pain in my tail. That's right, it was Punk Rat.

Suddenly, I spotted the little pest on the

shore. He must have been left behind when the boat took off.

"Don't move, Punk Rat!" I yelled. "It's dangerous! We'll come and pick you up."

"DON'T MOVE!!!"
"IT'S DANGEROUS!!!"

But at that moment, disaster struck. Punk Rat slipped on a wet rock. He tumbled into the water.

He disappeared into a menacing whirlpool.

A Dive...in the Icy Water!

A little voice inside my head began screaming at me. "Don't just stand there! Save him!" it yelled. I dove into the **wateR**. That's when the other little voice began screaming. It shrieked,

"Geronimo, are you crazy? You're not a swimmer. You can barely do two laps at the Cheddarville Y!"

ICY-COLD WATER soaked into my ears, my nose, even my throat. It blocked out the voices. All I could think about was **SAVING** Punk Rat.

I swam desperately toward him. I could

see his little head bobbing up and down in the waves. His little paws waved in the air. Up and down, wave. Up and down, wave. He looked like he was doing a perfect water ballet dance. I wondered if he had ever thought about taking lessons.

I was still thinking about water ballet when things went from bad to worse. Yep, Punk Rat went **UNDER**.

What could I do? I dove down after him.

It was dark under the water. I **COULD HARDLY SEE A THING**. Everything was so fuzzy. Everything was so blurry. *Maybe I need a new pair of glasses*, I thought. Then I realized I wasn't wearing glasses. I had lost them in the water!

Luckily, my paw felt **something**. It was Punk Rat's tail. I grabbed it. I pulled him up.

Someone threw me a life buoy from the boat. Then they pulled us in.

Cheesecake! We were saved!

You Are Not a Mouse... You Are a Hero!

The boat's captain patted me on the back. "*Nice going*, Mr. Stilton!" he exclaimed. Then he led the crowd in a chorus of cheers.

"HIP, HIP, HOORAY! HIP, HIP, HOORAY!"

they shouted.

A **large, beefy** tourist threw his paws around me. "That was beautiful," he squeaked. "Who would think a **scraggly** little rodent like you could do something like that?" He embraced me in a crunching hug. I felt all the bones in my body snapping. Then he accidentally stepped on my foot.

"OOOOOOOOOOOOOUUUUUCH!"

I screamed at the top of my lungs.

I quickly wrapped my foot in my nephew's bandanna.

Next, a little old lady mouse gave me a kiss. She had tears in her eyes.

"Bravo, young man! You are not a mouse...you are a hero!" she exclaimed.

While she was kissing me, the handle of her purse went into my eye.

"OOOOOOOOOOOOUUUUUCH!"

I screamed at the top of my lungs. My eye felt like it was on fire. I tied a handkerchief around my head to soak up the tears. Now I looked just like a PIRATE.

The whole class stared at me. I could tell they were impressed. Little mice love pirates.

"You're so lucky to have such a **COOL UNCLE**," Sakura told Benjamin.

My nephew **BEAMED** with pride.

Punk Rat and I were wet and shivering. A sailor wrapped us in a blanket. He gave us each a cup of **HOT** chocolate.

My paws were shaking so much I spilled mine all over me. "**OOOOOOOOUUUCH!**" I screamed at the top of my lungs.

Oh, when would this day come to an **END**?

OOOOOOOOOOOOOOUUUUUCH!

FRIENDS ... FUREVER!

When Punk Rat stopped shivering, he wrapped his paws around my neck.

"Thank you, Geronimo! You saved my life! I'm sorry I played all those dumb **tricks** on you," he gushed.

I tried to say something, but I couldn't squeak. I couldn't move. I couldn't breathe.

Punk Rat was squeezing my neck so tightly I was choking!

Friends furever!

At last, he let go. Then he shook my paw.

"**Friends...furever!**" the little rodent squeaked.

I gave him a weak smile. "**FUREVER**," I croaked, still gasping for breath.

The Adventure Seekers of Niagara Falls

Many people have come to Niagara Falls seeking fame and
adventure. Here are just a few of the most famous.

The first woman to hurl herself over the falls inside a wooden barrel was Annie Taylor, sixty-three years of age. She completed the feat in 1901, accompanied by her cat.

The first daredevil was Jean-François Gravelet, known as Blondin. In 1859 and 1860, he crossed the falls by walking on a rope stretched across the top.

After his first attempt failed because the authorities stopped him, Dave Munday succeeded in hurling himself over the falls in a barrel twice, once in 1985 and once in 1993.

Bobby Leach faced the falls in 1911. He locked himself in a steel barrel, but he was less lucky than Annie. He was in the hospital for six months with various broken bones.

Isn't It Magnificent, Geronimo?

Before we got off the boat, Benjamin spotted something floating in the water. It was my glasses. I reached over the side to fish them out, and...

SPLASH! I fell in.

I swam to shore. I was wet. I was cold. But I could see! I was in mouse heaven! I wondered if my glasses had missed me as much as I missed them.

We hiked back toward the camp.

We took a shortcut through the woods.

I looked around. The leaves on the trees were such beautiful colors—

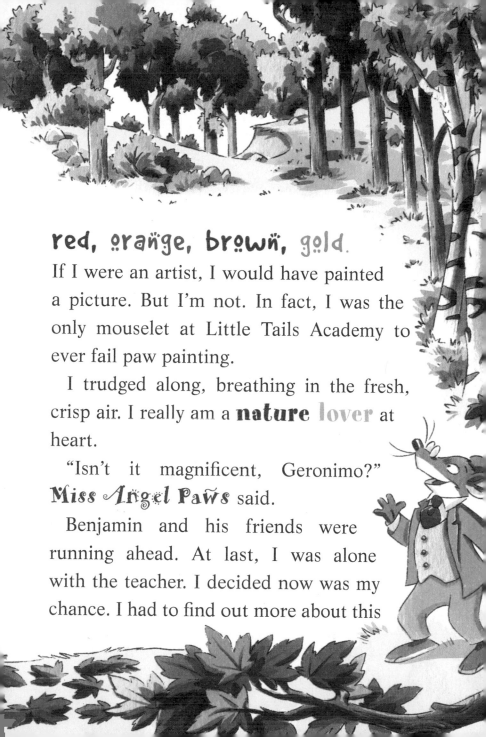

red, orange, brown, gold.

If I were an artist, I would have painted a picture. But I'm not. In fact, I was the only mouselet at Little Tails Academy to ever fail paw painting.

I trudged along, breathing in the fresh, crisp air. I really am a **nature** lover at heart.

"Isn't it magnificent, Geronimo?" **Miss Angel Paws** said.

Benjamin and his friends were running ahead. At last, I was alone with the teacher. I decided now was my chance. I had to find out more about this beautiful mouse. Maybe we could go out to dinner sometime. I wondered if she would like Le Squeakery. It's my favorite French restaurant.

"So, um, **Miss Angel Paws**," I began shyly. "Are you married?"

Miss Angel Paws shook her head. A big tear rolled down her fur. Then she collapsed in a fit of sobs.

Oh, why did I have such rotten luck with female mice? If they weren't crying, they were running away from me.

The teacher pulled herself together. "Sorry," she **sniffed**. "I am not married. But I was **IN LOVE** once, a long, long time ago...."

Carefully, she opened a locket that she wore around her neck. Inside was a whisker.

"This is his whisker," Miss Angel Paws explained. "It is all I have left of him. The last time I saw him, he was being chased by an angry cat. *I swore I would never fall in love again.*"

I sighed. What a *sad, sad story*. I felt bad for the whiskerless mouse. I felt bad for **Miss Angel Paws**. Right then, it began to rain. **The water poured down in buckets.**

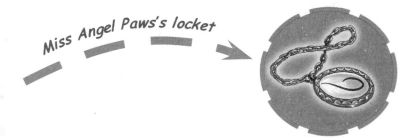

Miss Angel Paws's locket

Love Under a Cheese-Colored Umbrella

Suddenly, a mouse appeared out of nowhere. He was carrying a large **CHEESE-COLORED** umbrella.

"Please, allow me," he said *softly* to Miss Angel Paws. He held the umbrella over her head and smiled.

The two rodents stared at each other. They stared and stared. I wondered what the staring contest was all about. Then I noticed something. The mouse with the umbrella was missing a whisker. *Could it be*? I wondered.

Just then, the two mice clasped paws. "*It's you!*" they squeaked together.

Well, that answered that question. It was

Miss Angel Paws

Gentle Mouse

all pretty amazing. I mean, what were the chances **Miss Angel Paws** would find her lost *love* at Niagara Falls? That's like finding a cheese cracker in an overflowing garbage can. It takes more than just digging. It takes luck!

I was happy for the teacher. At least someone was having a lucky day. I, on the other paw, was not. The rain seeped into my fur. It dribbled down my whiskers. It poured into my ears. I was getting soaked. I could see the little mice huddled together in a dry cave up ahead.

Meanwhile, the two *love* mice had the cheese-colored umbrella to protect them. Not that they seemed to notice it was

raining. They looked like they were under some kind of *magic spell*. The kind that makes you forget where you are.

I sighed. I wished I were under a

magic spell.

Then I could forget I was standing outside in the middle of a torrential

RAINSTORM!

A REAL
GENTLE MOUSE

That night, we sat around a crackling campfire. It turned out Miss Angel Paws's friend was a forest ranger. His name was *Gentle Mouse*. I wanted not to like him. After all, I came on this trip just to spend more time with Miss Angel Paws. But how could I hate a rodent with a name like that?

Gentle Mouse knew a lot about *nature*. He showed us a maple leaf.

MAPLE SYRUP

The sap from maple trees can be boiled down and made into maple sugar or maple syrup. When winter turned into spring, Indigenous peoples would make V-shaped slashes in a maple tree trunk and collect the sap in a vessel. Then they would boil the sap down into sugar. The early European settlers learned this way of getting maple sugar from the Indigenous peoples.

MAPLE SYRUP

"From this **TREE**, we get **MaPLe SyRuP**," Gentle Mouse explained. He told the class how they could start their own collection of dried leaves.

HOW TO MAKE A COLLECTION OF DRIED LEAVES

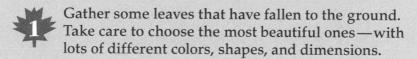

1 Gather some leaves that have fallen to the ground. Take care to choose the most beautiful ones—with lots of different colors, shapes, and dimensions.

2 As soon as you get home, clean the leaves well. To dry them, place them between two sheets of paper inside a thick book.

3 When the leaves are dry and flat, glue them in a notebook or put them in a photo album.

4 Next to each leaf, write its name and the date it was collected.

5 Near each leaf's common name, you can write its botanical name, which can be found in an encyclopedia or field guide.

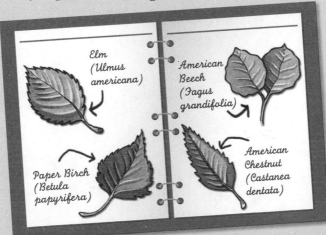

Elm (Ulmus americana)

American Beech (Fagus grandifolia)

Paper Birch (Betula papyrifera)

American Chestnut (Castanea dentata)

CHEEP...CHEEP... CHEEP...CHEEP...

The next MORNING, we went for a hike through the woods. I tried to keep up with the group, but I kept tripping over rocks and twigs. Did I mention I'm not much of a sports mouse?

Gentle Mouse pointed out the different plants along the way.

"This is a sugar maple. Its leaf is on the

Canadian flag," he explained. "This is a chestnut tree. Has anyone ever tried a **chestnut**?"

Just then, I saw two beady eyes blinking behind the bushes. "Look, a **fox**," Gentle Mouse whispered excitedly.

I gulped. I was okay with plants, but wild animals weren't exactly my cup of cheddar. They can be a little scary. No, make that downright **terrifying**!

I scampered past the **fox**.

Gentle Mouse was busy pointing out other

TREES AND THEIR LEAVES

1. Silver Maple
Acer saccharinum

2. Norway Maple
Acer platanoides

3. Red Maple
Acer rubrum

4. Vine Maple
Acer circinatum

5. Paper Birch
Betula papyrifera

6. American Chestnut
Castanea dentata

7. American Beech
Fagus grandifolia

8. American Elm
Ulmus americana

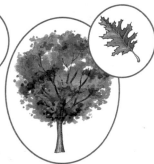

9. Red Oak
Quercus rubra

EVERGREENS

10. Pitch Pine
Pinus rigida

11. Red Pine
Pinus resinosa

12. Balsam Fir
Abies balsamea

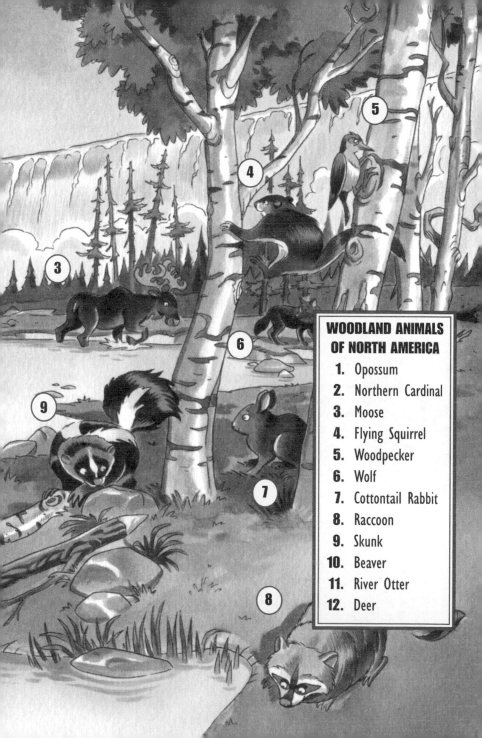

WOODLAND ANIMALS OF NORTH AMERICA

1. Opossum
2. Northern Cardinal
3. Moose
4. Flying Squirrel
5. Woodpecker
6. Wolf
7. Cottontail Rabbit
8. Raccoon
9. Skunk
10. Beaver
11. River Otter
12. Deer

animals. We saw a beaver, a raccoon, and even a deer with huge antlers.

I couldn't believe how many wild animals we came across. Suddenly, I heard a loud chirping. **Cheep! Cheep!**

I followed the chirping to an oak tree. A little bird was lying on the ground.

"Help! It's fallen and it can't get up!" I told Gentle Mouse. "What should we do?"

S.O.S. HOW TO GIVE FIRST AID TO A BIRD

1. When you find a little bird fallen to the ground, look for its nest around that area. Leave the bird alone and wait a little while....Its parents could come to claim it.

2. If there is no nest, pick the bird up from the ground gently.

3. If the bird is very small and still without feathers, you need to feed it, using a dropper.

4. If the bird has feathers, take a look at its beak. If it's short and strong, feed it grain seeds. If it's long and thin, feed it insects.

5. Keep the bird in a warm place that is similar to its nest, like a box with a woolen cloth.

6. As soon as the bird is able to fly, set it free. And remember, ask a parent or adult before touching any wild animal!

THE FOREST IS
ON FIRE!

Gentle Mouse showed us how to make a nest using a box and a towel. We found some seeds and fed them to the bird. It let out a happy chirp. Then it started SMOKING. Holey cheese! What was in those seeds? Then I realized the smoke wasn't coming from the bird. It was filling the air around us!

"FIRE!" someone screamed.

Gentle Mouse called for help on his cell phone. "HURRY! THE FOREST IS ON FIRE!" he cried. "Someone must have left a campfire burning. Send a plane right away!"

Gentle Mouse told everyone to STAY CALM. He divided us up into two teams.

The first team dug **FIRE TRENCHES.** "If we cut down all of the plants, the **FIRE** will have nothing to burn," Gentle Mouse explained.

The second team formed a long chain that ended at a nearby brook. The first mouse in line filled a pail with **water**. Then he passed it down the line. The last mouse in line threw the water on the flames.

 We worked like pack rats, but the heat was becoming unbearable. My fur was **scorched**. The smoke was making me choke.

Suddenly, a miracle happened. We heard the sound of engines. It was a plane carrying an enormouse tank filled with water! The plane dumped the water onto the flames and then left to pick up more water from the lake. We were saved! But

before we could celebrate, Gentle Mouse began **SHOUTING**. "Has anyone seen Miss Angel Paws?"

"I saw her running toward those bushes. I think she was trying to help a wounded fawn," Kay cried.

"Don't worry, Miss Angel Paws!" Gentle Mouse yelled. "I'll save you!"

He disappeared in a cloud of smoke. A few minutes later, he returned. He was carrying the teacher in his paws. "My hero," giggled Miss Angel Paws. "He saved the fawn, too!"

I felt a twinge of jealousy. Why couldn't I be someone's hero? Still, I had to admit, Miss Angel Paws and Gentle Mouse were a match made in mouse heaven.

95

HAVE I GOT A SURPRISE FOR YOU!

That night, the two **love mice** made an announcement. Can you guess what it was? Yes, they had decided to get married.

"**HOORAY**!" cried the class. Everyone was **so excited**. But they were even more excited when they heard that Miss Angel Paws and Gentle Mouse wanted to get married immediately. They had been missing each other for years. They didn't want to wait any longer.

"We can do it right here in Niagara Falls!" Miss Angel Paws squeaked.

We put our heads together to plan the ceremony. It would have to be pretty simple. There would be no **Wedding gown** or fancy wedding cake. After all, where could we get a dress and a cake in the middle of the wilderness?

I called my sister to ask for her advice. As I said, that mouse just loves a challenge.

An hour later, my cell phone **RANG**. It was Thea. "Hey, Gerry Berry, **have I got a surprise for you!**" she squeaked.

I **GULPED**. A surprise? From my sister? The last time she surprised me, she carpeted my whole apartment in **PINK CAT FUR**!

Flap, Flap, Flap...
Vrooooooommmmm!

Right at that instant, I heard a **strange** noise over my head.

I looked up and screamed.

A pink helicopter was circling above me.

Pink sugar-coated almonds rained down all around me.

Pink invitations with the bride's and groom's names on them flew through the air.

A bunch of thorny **pink** roses hit me in the snout. Youch!

So this was my sister's surprise. I was

relieved. I'd take a thorn in the snout over that awful **pink** carpeting any day.

I told everyone who the nutty mouse flying the plane was.

"My sister loves **pink**," I added.

Pink almonds

At that moment, an **ENORMOUSE pink** package struck me on the head. Before I fainted, I noticed a note on the side of the box. It said:

For Angel Paws and Gentle Mouse

Pink notes

When I came to, the others were busy opening **Thea's** package. No one gave me a second glance. I snorted. So much for mousely manners. It

Pink roses

was clear that all anyone cared about was the box.

What was inside? It was a full-length wedding dress and a tux. Now everyone was happy. Well, everyone except me, that is. A lump had formed on top of my head. It was the size of a mega-huge ball of *mozzarella*!

The surprise package

Congratulations!

Barbecue Time!

After the wedding ceremony, we headed back to the campsite. When we arrived we were overwhelmed by a delicious smell. I sniffed the air. Could it be? Yes, it smelled just like a **backyard barbecue**.

I ran toward the campsite. That's when I spotted a big poster leaning against a rock. It said:

BARBECUE!

COME ONE, COME ALL.
GET READY FOR THE BEST BARBECUE
THIS SIDE OF NIAGARA FALLS!

BROUGHT TO YOU BY THE
BEST CHEF IN THE WORLD!

I scratched my fur. There was only one rodent I knew who was that full of himself. There was only one rodent I knew who was that irritating…such a pain!

My cousin Trap!

Just then, a pair of whiskers emerged from behind a cloud of smoke. A *pot-bellied* rodent wearing a loud Hawaiian-print shirt stood behind a smoking grill. He waved a greasy spatula at me. "Yo, **Germeister**, what's squeaking?" he smirked. "Love the lump on your head. It's sooooo you!"

I rolled my eyes. Yep, it was my cousin Trap, all right. Have I mentioned he's a total pain in my tail?

I started to explain about the bump on my head when Trap interrupted me.

"Listen up, rodents!" he called. "You're about to taste the best cooking around. So don't drag your feet, it's time to eat. Now that you've found Trap, you can throw away your map. That's **TRAP**—

T as in *LOOK OUT, TONGUE, YOU'RE IN FOR A TREAT!*

R as in *READY OR NOT, HERE IT COMES!*

A as in *ASK ME IF I CAN COOK.*

P as in *PAY ATTENTION, THE NAME IS TRAP!*"

Yes, there is one thing you should know about my cousin. He's in love. No, not with another mouse. With himself!

Still, I had to admit his barbecue was DELICIOUS. I stuffed my snout like my uncle Cheesebelly at a *make-your-own-cheese-sundae buffet*.

After dessert, Thea took me on a helicopter ride over the **falls**. It really was a **SPECTACULAR** sight. Too bad I got sick on the way down. I knew I shouldn't have eaten **three pieces of cheesecake**!

THAT HIT THE SPOT!

Yum! Yum! Yum!

LITTLE MICE
AROUND THE WORLD

Finally, it was time to go home. We boarded
the plane headed for Mouse Island. It was
another long flight. The little mice climbed
all over me. Then they sang songs at the top
of their lungs. I didn't get one bit of rest.
Still, I was kind of *sad* when we landed. I
was going to miss those little rodents.

As we were waiting for our luggage, I
made an announcement. "You are all invited
to visit me at *The Rodent's Gazette,*" I told
the class. "You can see how we put the
newspaper together. You can see how a
book is made."

"HOORAY!" the little mice cheered.

Then Punk Rat grabbed my paw.

"I'm going to miss you, Mr. Geronimouse," he sobbed.

I patted his head.

"I'll miss you too, Punk Rat," I said. "Um, but remember, my name is *Geronimo, Geronimo Stilton*."

"**Of course**, Mr. Geronimity," Punk Rat squeaked.

I tried to remain calm. "It's Geronimo, Punk Rat," I repeated. "That's G-E-R-O-N-I-M-O."

Punk Rat smirked. "That's what I said, Mr. Geronimoose," he giggled.

I gave up. What else could I **DO**?

Punk Rat flung his paws around my neck. He really wasn't such a bad little mouse. In fact, he was just like lots of little mice around the world — *full of life and love and, oh, of course, cheese.*

TO TRAVEL...
IS BETTER THAN
TO ARRIVE

We headed for the airport exit. A school bus was waiting for Miss Angel Paws and her class. I waved good-bye. "I'll take a taxi home," I told them.

A line of cheese-colored cabs waited at the curb. But for some reason, my paws didn't want to budge. My bag felt like it weighed a ton. An overwhelming feeling of sadness came over me. It had been such an **exciting adventure**. And now it was over.

Just then, I remembered a line from one of my favorite authors. His name was

R. L. SQUEAKENSON

Robert Louis Squeakenson. Do you know him? He wrote a book called **TREASURE ISLAND**. Anyway, he said that TO TRAVEL IS BETTER THAN TO ARRIVE.

Well, I don't know if that is true all of the time. Usually, I am thrilled to get back to my comfy, cozy mouse hole. But this time, I still had the **travel bug** in me.

And so I did what any smart mouse would do. I turned around and headed right back into the airport. I, *Geronimo Stilton*, booked a trip to BLUE CHEESE ISLAND. I hear it's supposed to be beautiful there this time of year. Blue skies, blue waters, and lots and lots of blue cheese.

I couldn't wait to get there!

Geronimo's Joke Contest Winners!

Special thanks to all my mouse friends who sent me jokes! All the jokes were absolutely hilari-mouse. In fact, I laughed so hard, I almost broke my funny bone! Here are some of my favorites.

If a mouse lost his tail, where would he go to get a new one?
A re-tail store!
From Flannery in Washington State

When should a mouse carry an umbrella?
When it's raining cats and dogs!
From Caleb in Maryland

What animal is a tattletale?
A pig. It always squeals on you!
From Emily in Ohio

What's a mouse's favorite state?
Swissconsin!

Why do rodents like earthquakes?
Because they like to shake, rattle, and MOLE.
From Amanda in California

What's the tallest building in the world?
The library, of course! It has the most stories.

What do you call something easy to chew?
A ch-easy chew!

From Darianne in New Hampshire

What martial art does Geronimo Stilton like to practice?
Tai Cheese!

From Ryan in Texas

What happens to a cat when it eats a lemon?
It turns into a sourpuss!

From Tiffany in Florida

How do you make a tissue dance?
You put a little boogie in it.

From Zachery in New Jersey

What do you call a group of mice in disguise?
A mouse-querade party!

From the Freed family in Michigan

How does a mouse feel after a shower?
Squeaky clean!

From Ian in Washington State

What do you call a mouse that's the size of an elephant?
Enor-mouse!

From Parker

What's black and white and red all over?
The Rodent's Gazette! It's READ all over.

Don't miss a single fabumouse adventure!

Up Next:

Don't miss any of my adventures in the Kingdom of Fantasy!

THE KINGDOM OF FANTASY

THE QUEST FOR PARADISE:
THE RETURN TO THE KINGDOM OF FANTASY

THE AMAZING VOYAGE:
THE THIRD ADVENTURE IN THE KINGDOM OF FANTASY

THE DRAGON PROPHECY:
THE FOURTH ADVENTURE IN THE KINGDOM OF FANTASY

THE VOLCANO OF FIRE:
THE FIFTH ADVENTURE IN THE KINGDOM OF FANTASY

THE SEARCH FOR TREASURE:
THE SIXTH ADVENTURE IN THE KINGDOM OF FANTASY

THE ENCHANTED CHARMS:
THE SEVENTH ADVENTURE IN THE KINGDOM OF FANTASY

THE PHOENIX OF DESTINY:
AN EPIC KINGDOM OF FANTASY ADVENTURE

THE HOUR OF MAGIC:
THE EIGHTH ADVENTURE IN THE KINGDOM OF FANTASY

THE WIZARD'S WAND:
THE NINTH ADVENTURE IN THE KINGDOM OF FANTASY

THE SHIP OF SECRETS:
THE TENTH ADVENTURE IN THE KINGDOM OF FANTASY

THE DRAGON OF FORTUNE:
AN EPIC KINGDOM OF FANTASY ADVENTURE

THE GUARDIAN OF THE REALM:
THE ELEVENTH ADVENTURE IN THE KINGDOM OF FANTASY

THE ISLAND OF DRAGONS:
THE TWELFTH ADVENTURE IN THE KINGDOM OF FANTASY

Catch up on these special adventures!

The Hunt for the Golden Book

The Hunt for the Curious Cheese

The Hunt for the Secret Papyrus

The Hunt for the Hundredth Key

The Hunt for the Colosseum Ghost

THE JOURNEYS THROUGH TIME

1. THE JOURNEY THROUGH TIME

2. BACK IN TIME

3. THE RACE AGAINST TIME

4. LOST IN TIME

5. NO TIME TO LOSE

6. THE TEST OF TIME

Don't miss any of these exciting Thea Sisters adventures!

Thea Stilton and the
Dragon's Code

Thea Stilton and the
Mountain of Fire

Thea Stilton and the
Ghost of the Shipwreck

Thea Stilton and the
Secret City

Thea Stilton and the
Mystery in Paris

Thea Stilton and the
Cherry Blossom Adventure

Thea Stilton and the
Star Castaways

Thea Stilton: Big Trouble
in the Big Apple

Thea Stilton and the
Ice Treasure

Thea Stilton and the
Secret of the Old Castle

Thea Stilton and the
Blue Scarab Hunt

Thea Stilton and the
Prince's Emerald

Thea Stilton and the
Mystery on the Orient Express

Thea Stilton and the
Dancing Shadows

Thea Stilton and the
Legend of the Fire Flowers

Thea Stilton and the
Spanish Dance Mission

Thea Stilton and the
Journey to the Lion's Den

Thea Stilton and the
Great Tulip Heist

Thea Stilton and the
Chocolate Sabotage

Thea Stilton and the
Missing Myth

Thea Stilton and the
Lost Letters

Thea Stilton and the
Tropical Treasure

Thea Stilton and the
Hollywood Hoax

Thea Stilton and the
Madagascar Madness

Thea Stilton and the
Frozen Fiasco

Thea Stilton and the
Venice Masquerade

Thea Stilton and the
Niagara Splash

Thea Stilton and the
Riddle of the Ruins

Thea Stilton and the
Phantom of the Orchestra

Thea Stilton and the
Black Forest Burglary

Don't miss any of my fabumouse special editions!

THE JOURNEY TO ATLANTIS

THE SECRET OF THE FAIRIES

THE SECRET OF THE SNOW

THE CLOUD CASTLE

THE TREASURE OF THE SEA

THE LAND OF FLOWERS

THE SECRET OF THE CRYSTAL FAIRIES

THE DANCE OF THE STAR FAIRIES

ABOUT THE AUTHOR

Born in New Mouse City, Mouse Island, **GERONIMO STILTON** is Rattus Emeritus of Mousomorphic Literature and of Neo-Ratonic Comparative Philosophy. For the past twenty years, he has been running *The Rodent's Gazette,* New Mouse City's most widely read daily newspaper.

Stilton was awarded the Ratitzer Prize for his scoops on *The Curse of the Cheese Pyramid* and *The Search for Sunken Treasure.* He has also received the Andersen 2000 Prize for Personality of the Year. One of his bestsellers won the 2002 eBook Award for world's best ratling's electronic book. His works have been published all over the globe.

In his spare time, Mr. Stilton collects antique cheese rinds and plays golf. But what he most enjoys is telling stories to his nephew Benjamin.

Map of New Mouse City

1. Industrial Zone
2. Cheese Factories
3. Angorat International Airport
4. WRAT Radio and Television Station
5. Cheese Market
6. Fish Market
7. Town Hall
8. Snotnose Castle
9. The Seven Hills of Mouse Island
10. Mouse Central Station
11. Trade Center
12. Movie Theater
13. Gym
14. Catnegie Hall
15. Singing Stone Plaza
16. The Gouda Theater
17. Grand Hotel
18. Mouse General Hospital
19. Botanical Gardens
20. Cheap Junk for Less (Trap's store)
21. Aunt Sweetfur and Benjamin's House
22. Mouseum of Modern Art
23. University and Library
24. *The Daily Rat*
25. *The Rodent's Gazette*
26. Trap's House
27. Fashion District
28. The Mouse House Restaurant
29. Environmental Protection Center
30. Harbor Office
31. Mousidon Square Garden
32. Golf Course
33. Swimming Pool
34. Tennis Courts
35. Curlyfur Island Amousement Park
36. Geronimo's House
37. Historic District
38. Public Library
39. Shipyard
40. Thea's House
41. New Mouse Harbor
42. Luna Lighthouse
43. The Statue of Liberty
44. Hercule Poirat's Office
45. Petunia Pretty Paws's House
46. Grandfather William's House

Brigand's Isle

This way to the Rodent Straits

Pirate Ship of Cats

Tomcat Island

Hamster Islands

Blue Dolphin Bay

Coral Reefs

This way to the Mousific Ocean

Stray Cat Harbor

San Mouscisco

Cat's Claw Bay

Panther Archipelago

Swissville

Cheddarton

Mouseport

This way to the Ratlantic Ocean

Mousefort Beach

New Mouse City

Furflung Island

This way to the Sea of Mice

MOUSE ISLAND

N
W E
S

Map of Mouse Island

1. Main entrance
2. Printing presses (where the books and newspaper are printed)
3. Accounts department
4. Editorial room (where the editors, illustrators, and designers work)
5. Geronimo Stilton's office
6. Helicopter landing pad

THE RODENT'S GAZETTE